Joan Tate **Jock and the Rock Cakes**

Illustrated by Carolyn Dinan

 CHILDRENS PRESS, CHICAGO

Library of Congress Cataloging in Publication Data

Tate, Joan.
  Jock and the rock cakes.

  SUMMARY: Jock's cakes are so hard no one wants
to eat them.   But Loppy loves them.
  I.   Dinan, Carolyn.   II.   Title.
PZ7.T21125Jo5   [E]   75-40351
ISBN 0-516-03584-3

American edition published 1976 by
Regensteiner Publishing Enterprises, Inc.
All rights reserved. Printed in the U.S.A.
Published simultaneously in Canada.
First published 1973 by Knight books and
Brockhampton Press Ltd, Salisbury Road, Leicester
Printed in Great Britain by Cox & Wyman Ltd,
London, Fakenham and Reading
Second impression 1974
Text copyright © 1973 Joan Tate
Illustrations copyright © 1973 Brockhampton Press Ltd

"Can I make rock cakes?" says Jock one day.

"In the new mixer?" says Mom.

"Yes," says Jock.

"What do I do?" says Jock.

"Well, look in the cookbook," says Mom.

Jock gets the cookbook down from the shelf.

Then Jock puts flour and things into the mixer bowl.

"Turn it on," says Mom. "Slow, now."
But Jock turns the mixer on too fast.
"Turn it off!" says Mom. "It's much too fast."

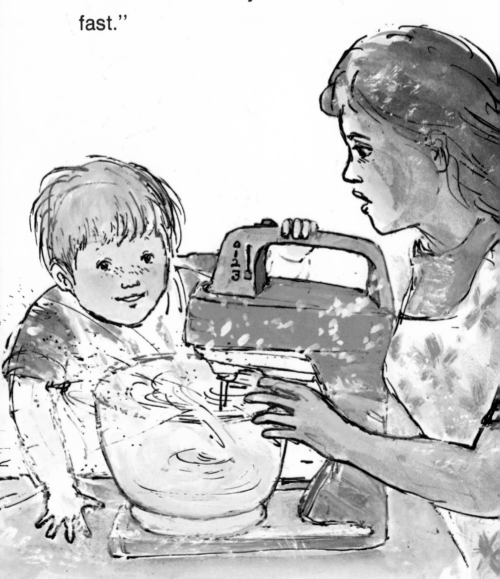

Jock looks funny with flour in his hair.
Mother is cross. But she looks funny, too.

Jock has to make more rock cakes.
Jock turns on the mixer—*slow*, this time.

Mom gets the rock cakes out of the oven. They look good.

The rock cakes are brown and hot. Jock bites one. It's good.

"Try one, Mom," says Jock.

"Not now, thanks," she says.

"Later."

Jock gives one to Dad. "Try one," he says. "I made them."

"You made them?" says Dad. "I didn't know you could make cakes."

"I made them in the new mixer," says Jock.

Dad eats the rock cake. He takes a
long time, but he eats it.

Later, Jock takes his rock cakes next
door to Jimmy's house.

"Here, Jimmy," he says. "Try one.
I made them."

"How?" says Jimmy.

"In Mom's new mixer," says Jock.

Jimmy bites a rock cake. He makes a funny face. "Ugh!" he says. "It's as hard as rock."

"Well," says Jock, "they *are* rock cakes."

Jock takes the rock cakes to
Grandmother's house.

He tells her about the new mixer.
She takes a rock cake and says thank
you.

"Very nice," Grandmother says. "Thank you, Jock."

But Jock sees that she doesn't eat all of it. "Oh," says Jock. "They don't like my rock cakes."

Jock takes the last rock cakes back to
his house. He doesn't know what to do
with them.

Loppy is in the garden. He is on his back with his feet up. He looks funny.

"Sit up, Loppy," says Jock.
Loppy sits up. He looks at Jock.

Jock gives Loppy a piece of rock cake.
Loppy eats it up at once. He looks at the
other pieces.

Jock gives Loppy *all* the rock cakes.
Loppy eats them *all* up. He likes rock
cakes.

Jock loves Loppy.